I can't sleep tonight. I'm too excited!
Because tomorrow . . .

Me, my mum and my big brother, Jamal, are going on holiday to see Grammy and Grampy. It feels as though we've been packing **FOREVER** but at last we're ready to go!

I'm gonna be:

fist-bumping with a turtle . . .

dancing with a dolphin . . .

high-fiving an octopus . . .

and surfing the waves like awesome Imani Wilmot.

DID YOU KNOW
Imani Wilmot created the first female surf competition in Jamaica!

As soon as we arrive, I give
Grammy and Grampy a **HUGE** hug.

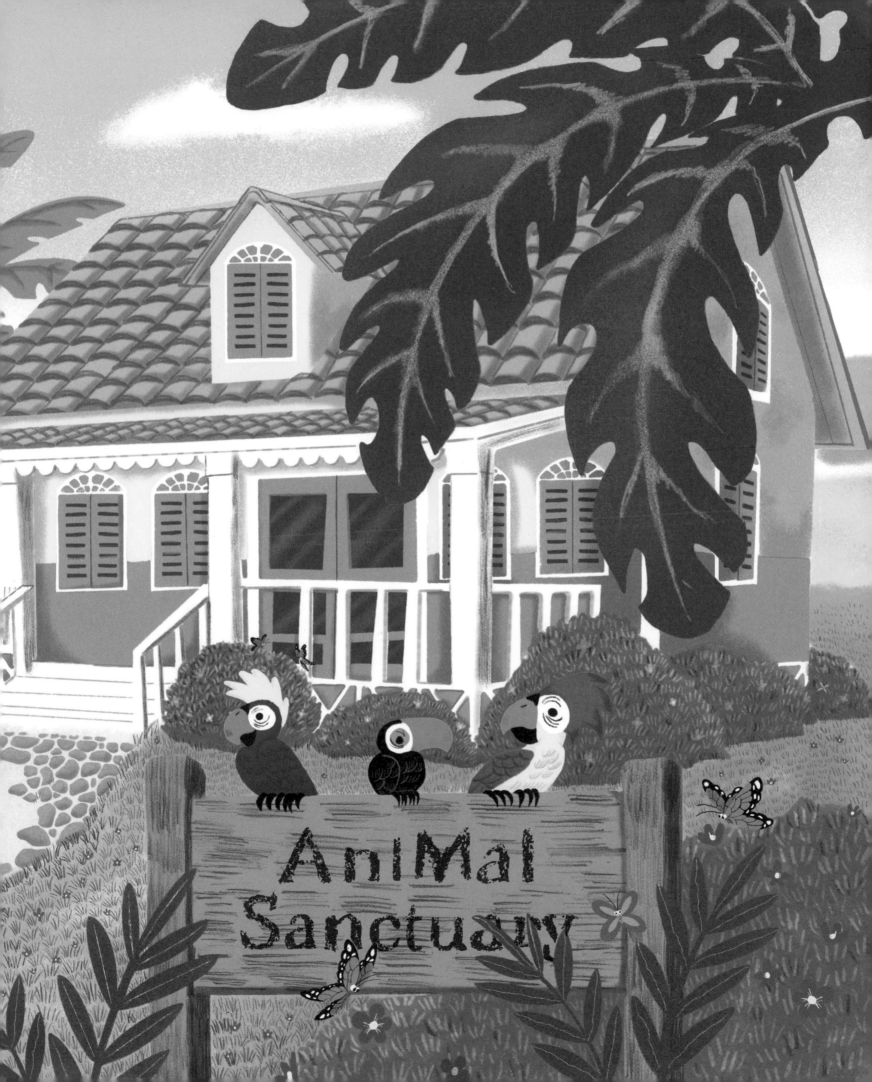

My grandparents are the best. They run a whale-watching tour and have an animal sanctuary at the back of their house.

I can't wait to help out!

Grampy tells me we never touch wild animals
unless they need to be rescued or cared for.

And then it's time to surf.
Grammy is really good!

Mum and I build a **HUGE** sandcastle!
Jamal is too busy to help . . .

OH NO! A baby turtle has washed up
to the shore, and it's all tangled in plastic.

I pick up the baby turtle gently and take her to Grammy and Grampy - they can fix this.

Grammy says she will do what she can and takes her back to the sanctuary.

"Plastic is ruining these islands, Rocket," says Grampy sadly.

"We save as many creatures as we can, but many stay away. People used to come here to see whales – but we haven't spotted one in a long time."

He leads me down the beach.

It feels as though there is more plastic than sand!

I feel really sad. We need
to **DO** something. But what?

The next day at the beach, there are people playing in the sand, swimming in the sea, eating ice lollies, but all I notice now is the plastic.

Surely they see it too?

I need to let **EVERYONE** know!

DID YOU KNOW

whales eat the plastic and it makes them sick?

DID YOU KNOW

nearly half the rubbish in the sea comes directly from careless people?

DID YOU KNOW

there are over 5.25 TRILLION pieces of plastic in the ocean?

Soon we have lots of new friends who want to help. It's a . . .

CLEAN-UP CREW!

As the day goes on, more and more people join in.
We spend the whole day cleaning the beach.

Even Jamal helps!

The **CLEAN-UP CREW** is amazing!

And soon the beach is . . .

CLE

AN!

But now what do we do with all the plastic we collected?

Theresa, one of the **CLEAN-UP CREW**, has a brainwave.

"My mum is an artist - we could get her to make something!"

Theresa's mum makes some awesome bins for the rubbish.

And the whole **CLEAN-UP CREW** makes the front pages and the TV news!

Island News

Clean Beach

Now no one will forget why we need to **CLEAN UP!**

Everyone on the island wants clean beaches.

Everyone on the island wants clean water.

Everyone on the island wants to save
the sea life and bring back the whales.

The next day, Grammy and Grampy have a barbecue for the whole **CLEAN-UP CREW**. The smell of Grammy's special sauce is wafting around the island.

And best of all, while everyone's talking and laughing and eating, Grampy and I release the turtle we rescued back into the sea and watch as she swims away.

She's all better now!

And I just know that one day the whales will come back.

DID YOU KNOW one day you are going to change the world, Rocket!

C N P!

Written by
Nathan Bryon

Illustrated by
Dapo Adeola

To my wonderful fiancée, Theresa, my incredible grandparents,
Ralph and Sylvia and Ann and Pat, who have always looked over me,
and to Phaedra for keeping the Rocket energy alive daily! - N.B.

Dedicated to my ever-amazing Nan, Rosaline Aderonke Tella,
who never lets me forget who I am - especially when it
feels like the rest of the world wants me to.
Love you like fried plantain. X - D.A.

PUFFIN BOOKS

UK | USA | Canada | Ireland | Australia | India | New Zealand | South Africa

Puffin Books is part of the Penguin Random House group of companies
whose addresses can be found at global.penguinrandomhouse.com.

Penguin
Random House
UK

First published 2020

001

Text copyright © Nathan Bryon, 2020
Illustrations copyright © Dapo Adeola, 2020

The moral right of the author and illustrator has been asserted

Printed in China
A CIP catalogue record for this book is available from the British Library

ISBN: 978-0-241-34589-4

All correspondence to: Puffin Books, Penguin Random House Children's
One Embassy Gardens, New Union Square
5 Nine Elms Lane, London SW8 5DA

MIX
Paper from
responsible sources
FSC® C018179
FSC
www.fsc.org